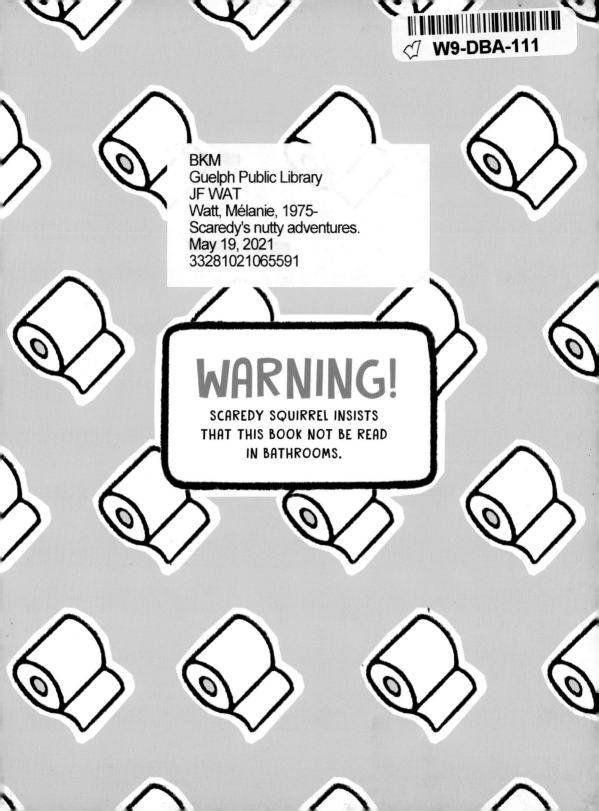

W9-DBA-111

BKM
Guelph Public Library
JF WAT
Watt, Mélanie, 1975-
Scaredy's nutty adventures.
May 19, 2021
33281021065591

WARNING!

SCAREDY SQUIRREL INSISTS
THAT THIS BOOK NOT BE READ
IN BATHROOMS.

READER SECURITY QUIZ

1. I HOLD BOOKS WITH...

HANDS ☐ (1 point)

SHARP CLAWS ☐ (0 points)

SLIMY TENTACLES ☐ (0 points)

2. SQUIRRELS ARE...

OVERRATED ☐ (0 points)

FUN TO CHASE ☐ (-1 point)

LOVABLE RODENTS ☐ (1 point)

3. I SMELL GOOD...

SORT OF ☐ (0 points)

ONLY ON SPECIAL OCCASIONS ☐ (0 points)

ALL YEAR LONG ☐ (1 point)

4. S.O.S. STANDS FOR...

SMALL ONION SOUP ☐ (0 points)

SAVE OUR SOULS ☐ (1 point)

SCAREDY ORVILLE SQUIRREL ☐ (1 point)

5.

OBSERVE THIS INKBLOT AND DESCRIBE WHAT YOU SEE.

ANSWER: AN INK SPOT THAT NEEDS TO BE SPOT-CLEANED IMMEDIATELY. (1 point)

6.

HAVE YOU BEEN IN CONTACT WITH ANY OF THESE INDIVIDUALS IN THE PAST 12 MONTHS?

PIRATES

(0 points)

BIGFOOT

(0 points)

GARY THE GERM

(-87 points)

CONGRATULATIONS!
IF YOUR TOTAL POINTS ARE BETWEEN 1 AND 6,
YOU CAN SAFELY PROCEED TO THE NEXT PAGE.

Scaredy Squirrel

In a Nutshell

BY MELANIE WATT

tundra

JF
WAT

FOR XAVIER &
(WHO DRIVE ME NUTS AT TIMES, BUT WHOM I'M

Text and illustrations copyright © 2021 by Melanie Watt

Tundra Books, an imprint of Penguin Random House Canada Young Readers, a division of Penguin Random House of Canada Limited

All rights reserved. The use of any part of this publication reproduced, transmitted in any form or by any means, electronic, mechanical, photocopying, recording, or otherwise, or stored in a retrieval system, without the prior written consent of the publisher — or, in case of photocopying or other reprographic copying, a licence from the Canadian Copyright Licensing Agency — is an infringement of the copyright law.

Library and Archives Canada Cataloguing in Publication

Title: Scaredy Squirrel in a nutshell / Melanie Watt.
Names: Watt, Mélanie, 1975- author, illustrator.
Identifiers: Canadiana (print) 20200291416 | Canadiana (ebook) 20200291424
ISBN 9780735269576 (hardcover) | ISBN 9780735269583 (EPUB)
Subjects: LCGFT: Graphic novels.
Classification: LCC PN6733.W38 S23 2021 | DDC j741.5/971—dc23

Simultaneously published in the United States of America by Random House Books for Young Readers, an imprint of Penguin Random House LLC

Edited by Tara Walker and Michelle Nagler
Designed by Melanie Watt
The artwork in this book was rendered in charcoal pencil and colored digitally in Photoshop.
The text was set in Garden Gnome.

Printed and bound in China

www.penguinrandomhouse.ca

1 2 3 4 5   25 24 23 22 21

Penguin
Random House
tundra | TUNDRA BOOKS

NUTTY CONTENTS

CHAPTER 1
SAFE AND SOUND

SCAREDY SQUIRREL
WATCHES OVER HIS
NUT TREE.

9

A FEW TRESPASSERS SCAREDY SQUIRREL IS AFRAID COULD DROP BY:

MUST UPROOT TREE!

MAMMOTHS

MUST POKE HOLES IN TREE!

WOODPECKERS

ALIENS

LUMBERJACKS

CATS

TERMITES

THIS PAGE IS BLANK FOR SUPERSTITIOUS REASONS.

MUST
JINX
TREE!

SCAREDY SQUIRREL BEGAN PROTECTING
HIS NUT TREE AT AN EARLY AGE.

WARNING!
CUTE FACTOR MIGHT BE
OVERWHELMING FOR SOME.

WOODEN
TRAIN
SIDETRACKS
TERMITES

TRAFFIC CONE
FENDS OFF
ALIENS

15

AS SCAREDY'S NUT TREE GREW,
SO DID HIS SAFETY MEASURES.

DISCO BALL

GARDEN GNOME

PROS:

OBJECTS DISTRACT TRESPASSERS

CONS:

OBJECTS ATTRACT DUST, AND DUST GATHERS...

DUST BUNNIES

(ACCORDING TO SCAREDY SQUIRREL)

LUCKILY, SCAREDY KNOWS HOW TO KEEP THINGS CLEAN WITH A . . .

SCUBA MASK

DUST-REPELLENT SUIT

PAIR OF
RUBBER GLOVES

VACUUM

SCAREDY SQUIRREL
VACUUMS...

PLAID
SALE!!!

(IN THE CITY)

AND VACUUMS...

AND VACUUMS...

WHEN SUDDENLY...

THE VACUUM CLOGS!

21

A FEW ITEMS THAT COULD BE AT THE BOTTOM OF THIS:

A. WOOL

B. FEATHERS

C. BOLTS AND SCREWS

D. MUSTACHES

E. HAIRBALLS

F. WOOD CHIPS

HE MUST UNCLOG
THIS VACUUM BEFORE
THE DUST SETTLES IN!

23

SCAREDY'S SWIFT UNCLOGGING PLAN

STEP 1: PANIC

STEP 2: SLIDE DOWN VACUUM

STEP 3: LIFT VACUUM NOZZLE

STEP 4: UNCLOG IT WITH PLUNGER

STEP 5: HURRY BACK UP TREE

STEP 6: RESUME VACUUMING

DO NOT STEP ON GROUND

MAYDAY!
Shedding woolly mammoths like to scratch their behinds on icy, snow-covered trees!

MOVE FAST!
Lumberjacks may be twirling their mustaches near tempting sign.

PLAID SALE!!!

(IN THE CITY)

LOOK OUT! Aliens want to beam up everything! If spaceship hovers too long, loose bolts, nuts and screws can drop to the ground!

I AM HERE.

ALERT! Woodpeckers cannot stand the glare of mirrors. If they come a-knocking, feathers will fly!

CAREFUL! Wooden train is packed with wood chips and dizzy termites.

REMEMBER! This sturdy security guard is on duty!

DANGER! Stepping on a hairball can lead to a mushy mess!

CLOG IS IN HERE.

ACHOO!

NOTE TO SELF: IF ALL ELSE FAILS, PLAY DEAD FOR 2 HOURS, THEN DUST YOURSELF OFF!

AS PLANNED,
SCAREDY SLIDES
DOWN THE VACUUM.

THEN HE CAREFULLY
LIFTS UP THE NOZZLE...

AND DISCOVERS SOMETHING MORE TERRIFYING
THAN HE HAD EVER IMAGINED...

SCAREDY RACES BACK UP THE TREE
AND KNOCKS DOWN THE VACUUM...

WHICH KNOCKS OFF THE
DISCO BALL...

WHICH KNOCKS THE GNOME...

WHICH KNOCKS INTO THE TREE...

AND KNOCKS OUT EVERY SINGLE NUT!

SCAREDY SQUIRREL PANICS AND...

PLAYS DEAD.

YIPPEE!!! FOUND MY EARMUFFS!

2 HOURS LATER...

CHAPTER 2
OUT AND ABOUT

SCAREDY SQUIRREL
WANTS TO EAT A NUT.

BUT TO GET A NUT,
HE MUST SET FOOT ON
DANGEROUS GROUND.

A FEW POSSIBLE RUN-INS THAT MAKE THIS A RISKY MOVE:

ROCKS

CACTI

PUDDLES

BURROWS AND . . .

THE BUNNY
(ACCORDING TO SCAREDY SQUIRREL)

MUST MAKE EYE CONTACT WITH SQUIRREL!

WEARS EARMUFFS THAT CLOG VACUUMS

ASKS IF ALL IS OKAY

STILL ATTACHED TO AN ADORABLE POM-POM TAIL

63% SURE IT KNOWS GARY

Scaredy's TO-DO List:

☑ Wait an entire year for new nuts to grow in.

Fall

Summer

Spring

Winter

☑ In the meantime, order takeout!

A FEW SNACKS ON SCAREDY'S DINING PLAN:

THE EARLY SQUIRREL SPECIAL!

NUT OVER EASY

NO HOT PEPPERS!

NUT TACO

GRILLED AT A SAFE DISTANCE!

NUT KEBAB

BEST INVENTION SINCE SLICED ALMONDS!

NUT SANDWICH

FAST AND EASY FOR RODENTS WHO ARE NEVER ON THE GO!

NUT SMOOTHIE

PLEASING TO THE EYE AND MOUTH!

NUT SUSHI

A HEALTHY CHOICE!

NUT SALAD

HELLO, MAY I PLACE AN ORDER, PLEASE?

NUTTY FOOD TRUCK

SORRY! WE ARE CLOSED TODAY.

FLAT TIRE

FORTUNATELY, THIS SQUIRREL ALWAYS HAS A PLAN B...

PLAN B:

PIZZA

31 MINUTES LATER...

HMMM. NUT TREE? WHERE?

SCAREDY'S DELIVERY GETS DROPPED OFF...

IN THE WRONG SPOT!

PIZZA

PILE OF NUTS, CLOSE ENOUGH!

PLAID SALE, HERE I COME!

PIZZA

ANY WAY YOU SLICE IT, SCAREDY WILL HAVE TO SET FOOT ON THE GROUND. THIS IS RISKY ON A WHOLE OTHER LEVEL!

SCAREDY'S GROUND-LEVEL GET-UP:

SAFETY HELMET

T. REX GRABBER TOOL

ELBOW PADS

KNEE PADS

STILTS

DO NOT STEP ON GROUND

1. MARCH TOWARD THE PIZZA BOX
2. OPEN BOX WITH GRABBER TOOL
3. GRAB A SLICE WITH GRABBER TOOL
4. HURRY BACK UP TREE, EAT SLICE
5. REPEAT STEPS UNTIL BOX IS EMPTY

NOTE TO SELF: IF IT ALL FALLS FLAT, PLAY DEAD!

SCAREDY STARTS MARCHING...

HE APPROACHES THE PIZZA...

AND LEANS IN TO OPEN THE BOX WHEN...

SCAREDY SCRAMBLES TO SAFETY AND PLAYS DEAD.

49

2 HOURS LATER...

CHAPTER 3
STRANGER DANGER

SCAREDY SQUIRREL
IS HUNGRY FOR
ANSWERS.

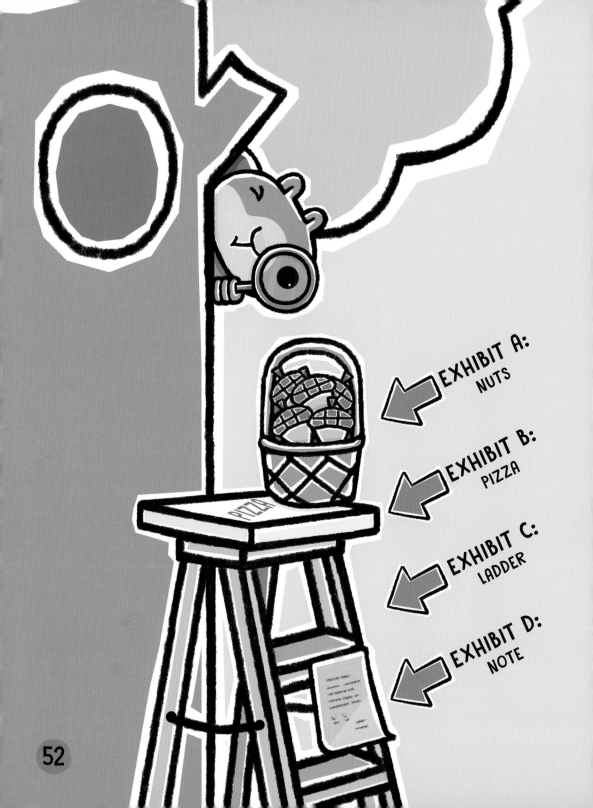

EXHIBIT A:
NUTS

EXHIBIT B:
PIZZA

EXHIBIT C:
LADDER

EXHIBIT D:
NOTE

TO AVOID PAPER CUTS,
SCAREDY PUTS ON
HIS OVEN MITTS.

Hi, up there.
Sorry if I scared
you earlier.
Maybe we can
meet halfway?

☐ ☐
Yes No

Ivy
(your friendly neighbor)

SCAREDY SQUIRREL
IS STUMPED.
HE MUST CALCULATE
THE RISKS BEFORE
HE CAN ANSWER IVY.

53

 # RISKS:

1. Ivy might be
poisonous!
(name makes me itchy)

DANGER!

2. Ivy might really be
Gary in disguise!

HEE! HEE! HEE!
'TWAS ME
ALL ALONG!

3. Ivy might be a
spy searching
for my classified
information!

TOP SECRET!

GOTCHA,
SQUIRREL!

4. Ivy and I might
have **nothing**
in common!!!

AWKWARD!

BENEFITS:

1. Ivy is NOT a dust bunny.

2. Ivy is kind to my tree.

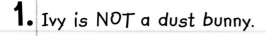

3. Ivy is friendly to me.

LET'S CHAT!

4. Ivy unclogs vacuums.

5. Ivy is helpful.

PIZZA

6. Ivy smiles.

7. Ivy is peaceful.

8. Ivy has impeccable handwriting!
(a rare skill nowadays)

AFTER CAREFUL THOUGHT, SCAREDY CONCLUDES THAT THE REALISTIC BENEFITS OUTWEIGH THE UNLIKELY RISKS.

IN A NUTSHELL:
IVY = SAFE

SCAREDY HANDS OVER HIS ANSWER.

OKAY... A BIT STRANGE. BUT WORKS FOR ME!

☑ Yes

Let's meet halfway and split a pizza at half past 5!

A FEW LAST-MINUTE DETAILS SCAREDY MUST HANDLE BEFORE 5:30 P.M.:

MEASURING TAPE

NAME TAGS

TOOTHPASTE

RADIO

HAND SANITIZER

NAPKINS

4:52 P.M. SCAREDY MEASURES THE HALFWAY SPOT.

5:07 P.M. HE PREPARES AN ID VERIFICATION TEST.

5:09 P.M. HE BRUSHES HIS TEETH.

5:12 P.M. HE PLAYS ELEVATOR MUSIC AND WAITS.

SCAREDY AND IVY FINALLY MEET FACE-TO-FACE (SORT OF).

HELLO! MY NAME IS SCAREDY SQUIRREL. PLEASE PICK THE NAME TAG THAT BEST SUITS YOU!

HI, SCARE-DY! THAT EXPLAINS A LOT!

IVY! MAY I OFFER YOU A SPRITZ OF HAND SANITIZER, 9 NAPKINS AND A SLICE OF PIZZA?

SURE!

SCAREDY EAGERLY OPENS THE BOX...

2 MINUTES LATER, THEY REALIZE...

OKAY, SO THEY DON'T HAVE THAT MUCH IN COMMON.
BUT SCAREDY IS STILL GLAD HE MET A NEW FRIEND!

SCAREDY AND IVY HAVE A PICNIC...

THEY CHAT...

WHEN I'M NOT IN MY BURROW, I GARDEN AND ENJOY READING ALL SORTS OF BOOKS!

WHEN I'M NOT IN MY NUT TREE...I PANIC. I ENJOY READING WARNING SIGNS AND EXPIRATION DATES!

AND THEY WATCH THE SUNSET.

...PIZZA!!!
WE FORGOT THE PIZZA! IVY! LET'S HURRY UP AND CATAPULT IT OUT INTO SPACE BEFORE IT ATTRACTS A HERD OF HUNGRY ANCHOVY-LOVING FLAMINGOS!!

HELLO MY NAME IS Scaredy

HELLO

OR...
WE COULD JUST CALL MY FRIEND TIM!

[crickets chirping]

HELLO

TIM LOVES ANCHOVIES! HE ADORES TREES! DON'T WORRY, SCAREDY. YOU'LL BOTH GET ALONG SO WELL!!!

TIM IS SHORT FOR TIMOTHY, RIGHT?

UH... NOT EXACTLY?

HELLO MY NAME IS Scaredy

HELLO MY NAME IS Timothy

TIMBER

(ACCORDING TO SCAREDY SQUIRREL)

THE END

FAQ

(FREQUENTLY ASKED QUESTIONS)

Q1 — SCAREDY, WILL YOU BE BACK WITH NEW NUTTY ADVENTURES?

S.O.S.: YES!!! I have plenty to be afraid of ... like Vikings, clams, yetis, bookworms and Gary.

MUST POKE SQUIRREL!

Q2 — SCAREDY, WHO'S THIS GARY YOU KEEP MENTIONING?

S.O.S.: A clingy germ rival who dates from waaay back.

GA-GA GRRR!

Q3 — WHERE CAN I FIND A SCAREDY SQUIRREL BOBBLEHEAD?

S.O.S.: Hopefully, nowhere!!!
Just the thought makes me dizzy!

SORRY TO INTERRUPT, BUT IS THERE ANY PIZZA LEFT?

Q4 — SCAREDY, WHY AREN'T YOU LIKE A TYPICAL TREE SQUIRREL?

S.O.S.: Because I'm not a typical tree squirrel — I'm atypical!
And that's what makes my adventures so incredibly fun!

Q5 — SCAREDY, CAN YOU LIST ALL OF YOUR PICTURE BOOKS?

S.O.S.:
- Scaredy Squirrel
- Scaredy Squirrel Makes a Friend
- Scaredy Squirrel at the Beach
- Scaredy Squirrel at Night
- Scaredy Squirrel Has a Birthday Party
- Scaredy Squirrel Goes Camping
...and more to come!

WATCH OUT FOR PAPER CUTS!